KU-350-639

Foybel

the baby dragon

PHILLIP COOTE

with illustrations by

BRIAN GOLD

papa books

To Kieran

Published by papa books
in conjunction with Blacker Publishing
info@blackerdesign.co.uk

ISBN 1-897739-26-5

Designed by Blacker Design

Printed and bound in China for Compass Press

Foybel the baby dragon
Who was such a lovely little chap.
Kissed and loved his mummy
When he sat upon her lap.

One day his mummy Roberta,
Who loved him very much,
Said 'You must learn to breathe
fire
Or you can't have any lunch'.

But he could not breathe out fire.
Even blowing hard and strong
He only managed a puff of smoke
Though he tried the whole day long.

And so his mummy Roberta
Said 'There is no other way.
We must go and see the wizard
And we'll leave without delay'.

They packed some coal and
some biscuits,
Some trousers and some shoes,
Washed their wings and their
faces.
There was no time to lose.

Roberta stretched her wings
And asked Foybel to do the same.
But Foybel wasn't listening
For he was playing a game.

Said Roberta 'Now Foybel
Please do as you are told.
Come and stand at the window
And let your wings unfold'.

Foybel came to the window
And held his mum's hand tight,
Looked to the ground from the window
And said to her 'I am fright!'

'Just follow me.' Roberta said
'I will show you how it is done.
Stretch your wings as I do
And take a little run.'

'Then give a little jump,
Stretch your wings and start
to flap.
You'll begin to fly as I do
You're a clever little chap.

Stretch your wings and start to flap ...

'How do we know where we
are going?'
Asked Foybel of his mum
'We just keep going this way
And follow our nose to the sun.'

'After a day and an hour,
Keeping the sun in sight,
Through the forest we shall run.
Swooping left and right.'

'Then we get to the mountains
And to the golden cave.
There we will find the Wizard,
We must be very brave.'

'Why does he live in a golden cave?'
Little Foybel said to his mummy.
'I am not really sure' she said
'I think it's a little funny.'

Said little Foybel to his mum.
'And why do we have to be brave?'
Roberta replied 'Because he's a wizard
And lives in a golden cave.'

'What do you think he'll look like?
And how will he be dressed?'
'I think in a heavy long brown robe
A gold star on his chest.'

The pilot of a passing plane could not believe his eyes ...

'Foybel you ask too many questions.'
Said Roberta who was now getting cross.
'But Mummy I just want some answers
And what is dental floss?'

As they flew to see the wizard
They saw some wondrous things.
They passed lots and lots of birds
And big planes that flew on wings.

The pilot of a passing plane
Could not believe his eyes.
He was so very startled
Seeing dragons in the skies.

At last they saw the mountains
In the distance to the south.
But still poor little Foybel
Breathed no fire from his mouth.

Roberta said to Foybel
'We have flown a very long way.
Would you like to take a rest
And stay here for the day?'

'Oh yes!' said Foybel to his mum
'That's a very good idea.
Can we stop this instant?'
'Of course, we could rest right here.'

Would you like to take a rest ...

They landed in the friendly wood
In a large green open space.
Roberta made a bed of moss
And washed little Foybel's face.

Foybel said 'I am hungry
What can we have to eat?'
'We'll pick some blue berries'
'Oh yes what a scrumptious treat'.

They lay down on their bed of moss.
Foybel went straight to sleep.
Roberta covered Foybel up
He slept without a peep.

Foybel and his mummy
Woke with the sun in their face.
Roberta called out to Foybel,
'This is a wondrous place.'

'But now it's time that we flew on
To the wizard in his cave of gold.
'We'll not be too long getting there
It's there we must be bold.'

Roberta took little Foybel's hand
Into the sky they flew,
And after flying for some time
The mountains came in view.

'Where is the wizard's golden cave?'
Asked Foybel of his mum.
'There it is ahead of us
Our journey's almost done.'

'Yes I can see it Mummy,
But where can we land?'
'There is a small spot by the lake
A little patch of sand.'

Where is the Wizards golden cave ...?

They flew down through the clouds
And landed on the sand.
Roberta said, 'Now fold your wings
You must look very grand.'

They trampled up a rocky path
To the Wizard's golden cave.
And there they found the Wizard
Looking rather grave.

The wizard saw them coming.
He spoke in a deep gruff tone
'Please state your names', the wizard said.
'I assume you've come alone'

'My name is Roberta'
Said the dragon so polite.
'And this is my son Foybel
Can you put him right?'

'Why what seems to be his problem?'
Asked the Wizard rubbing his head.
'He just cannot breathe out fire',
Roberta sadly said.

'Well' said the wizard kindly.
'It seems quite strange and odd,
You had better come in quickly,
Take a seat upon this log.'

They walked into the golden cave
Through a large wooden door.
Roberta looked around the walls
Amazed by what she saw.

The walls were covered in gold.
A blue diamond caught the light.
The wizard asked would they like
some food
And would they stay the night?

'Do you think you can help my son?'
Asked Roberta sounding worried.
The wizard muttered 'It's a
difficult case,
And one that can't be hurried.'

The wizard looked at Foybel.
'Please come and sit by me.
I must ask you some questions
Then we'll see what we will see.'

'Now tell me little dragon,
What happens when you blow?'
Foybel cried 'There's just no flame
And the reason I don't know.'

Roberta whispered 'I am so
troubled,
For dragons must breathe flame.
My Foybel is a lovely chap
It's such a great, great shame.'

The walls were covered in gold ...

The wizard looked at Foybel,
He rubbed his long grey beard.
And after many minutes
Exclaimed. 'It's as I feared!'

'Foybel's hitherall is not growing.'
Said the wizard with a puzzled look.
'Is that serious?', asked Foybel's mum.
'I will check in my wizard's spell
book.'

The wizard took a large brown book
From a very dusty shelf.
Going through it page by page,
He muttered to himself.

'Hand me that large cauldron!'
Shouted the wizard ever so loud.
'I am going to make a potion.
I will start with this white cloud.'

'We'll need to build a roaring fire
To get the cauldron hot.
We will put in all the ingredients
And mix them in this pot.'

I am going to make
a potion ...

'We need to catch a rainbow
And then some flakes of snow.
We will also need a moonbeam,
I know just where to go.'

The wizard went out from the cave
To catch the things on his list.
He returned with all he needed
Not a single one was missed.

And so Roberta and the wizard
Got busy straight away.
Mixing up all the ingredients
The wizard began to say ...

We need to catch a rainbow ...

Some words from his big brown spell book.
The potation boiled in the pot
Roberta asked 'More moonbeams?'
'No' said the wizard. 'That's the lot.'

Slowly the mixture thickened
Until it took on a shape.
The wizard murmured with excitement
And his mouth began to gape.

Slowly the mixture thickened

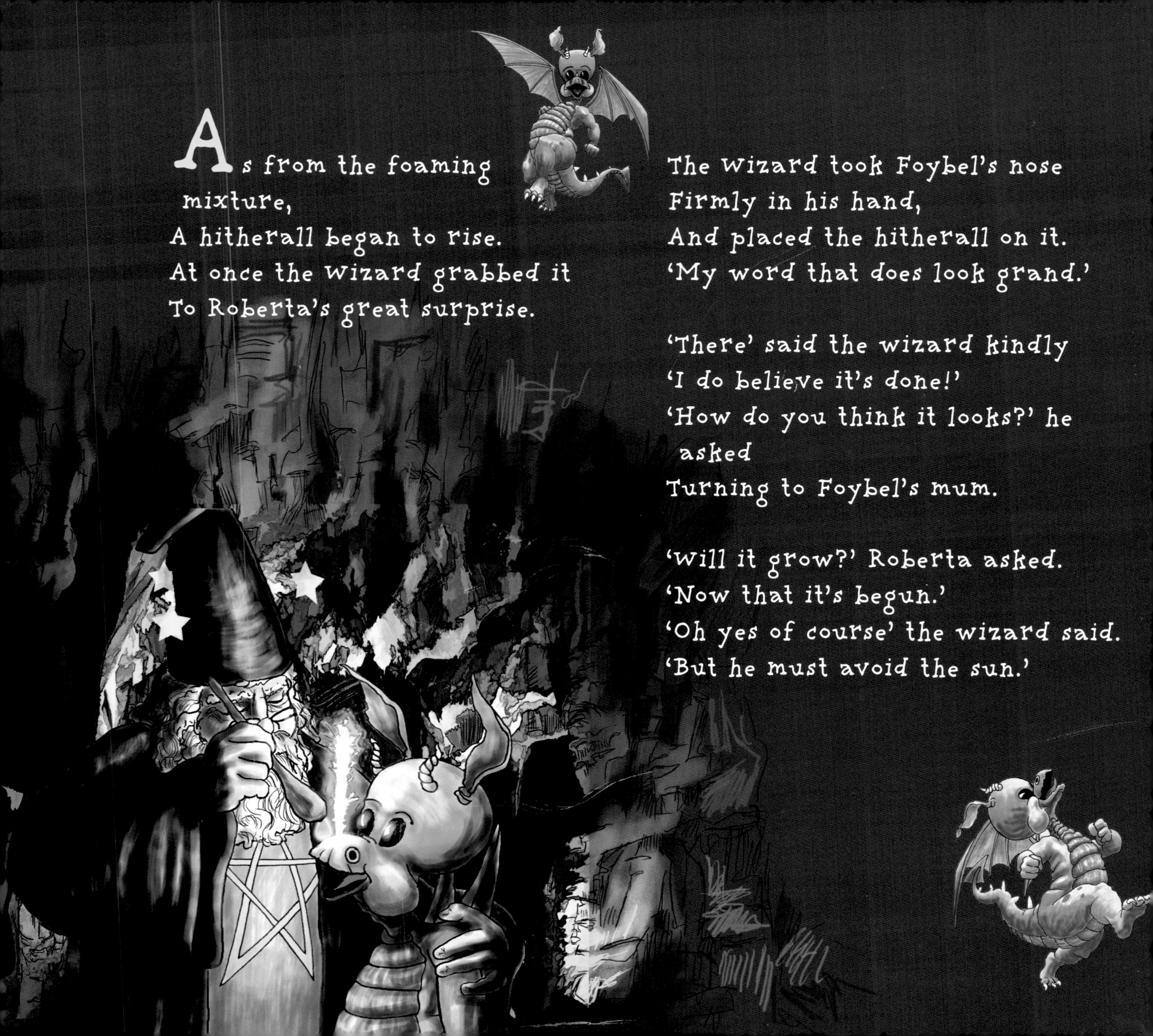

As from the foaming mixture,
A hitherall began to rise.
At once the Wizard grabbed it
To Roberta's great surprise.

The Wizard took Foybel's nose
Firmly in his hand,
And placed the hitherall on it.
'My word that does look grand.'

'There' said the wizard kindly
'I do believe it's done!'
'How do you think it looks?' he asked
Turning to Foybel's mum.

'Will it grow?' Roberta asked.
'Now that it's begun.'
'Oh yes of course' the wizard said.
'But he must avoid the sun.'

'There' said the wizard
'I do believe it's done!'

'When could we set off for
home?'
'You can leave tomorrow.'
'But, do you have some transport.
Which we could kindly borrow?'

'Hum, do I have some transport?
What would you be looking for?
I don't have bike or a motorcar.
But I might have a flying door!'

'A flying door?' exclaimed Roberta
'It's been out of use for an age.
One or two parts are broken,
And it's lacking a fuel gauge.'

'Well all right' Roberta said.
'If you think you can get it to go.
We would like to leave in the
morning.
Before it starts to snow.'

'A flying door?' exclaimed Roberta?

So climbing on the flying door,
And waving the wizard goodbye,
Foybel and his mum went home.
Flying oh so high!

Miss Poddletop

Furbog

Miss Springly

Foglet

Sir Joseph Yellowboots

Mr Blinky

Colonel Krunken

The Three Poilus

Diggerwise

Oren

Mrs Twitchnose